MW01087535

Taking Care of the
EARTH

Kids in Action

Taking Care of the
EARTH
Kids in Action

By **Laurence Pringle**

Illustrated by Bobbie Moore

Boyds Mills Press

Published by Caroline House
Boyds Mills Press, Inc.
A Highlights Company
815 Church Street
Honesdale, Pennsylvania 18431
Printed in Mexico

Publisher Cataloging-in-Publication Data
Pringle, Laurence.
    Taking care of the earth : kids in action / written by Laurence Pringle ;
illustrated by Bobbie Moore.—1st ed.
[64]p. : ill. ; cm.
Summary : A look at the ways in which kids care for the earth through
environmental projects and actions.
Hardcover ISBN 1-56397-326-X   Paperback ISBN 1-56397-634-X
1. Environmental protection—Juvenile literature. 2. Citizen
participation—Juvenile literature. [1. Environmental protection.
2. Citizen participation] I. Moore, Bobbie, ill. II. Title.
363.7 / 0525—dc20   1996   AC
Library of Congress Catalog Card Number 95-76352

Book designed by Jean Krulis
The text of this book is set in 12-pt Berkeley Book
The illustrations are done in black and white pencil.

Hardcover   10 9 8 7 6 5 4 3
Paperback   10 9 8 7 6 5 4 3 2

CONTENTS

"Never doubt that a small group of concerned people
can change the world.
Indeed, it's the only thing that ever has."

Margaret Mead

Taking Care by Taking Action

All over the United States, in Canada, and in other countries, young people are taking action to improve and protect the environment in which we all live:

*In Michigan, elementary students staged a musical and raised money to buy part of a rain forest in Costa Rica.

*Sixth-graders in Wyoming "adopted" part of a creek. They slowed down erosion along the creek's banks and planted trees and shrubs to attract wildlife.

*Students in Nebraska, New Jersey, Arizona, and many other states have helped start recycling programs in their schools.

We often hear discouraging news about the environment at school and from television and other news media. Some environmental problems are local, while others may affect everyone on earth. People are concerned about vanishing wildlife, growing mountains of trash, and the warming of the earth's atmosphere.

Environmental problems can be complex. But they can be solved when many people, young and old, take action. There *are* things that can be done to protect our land, air, water, and wildlife. This book gives specific details about some helpful projects and tells how thousands of young people are taking better care of our home, the earth.

1

Planting Trees

Kids have planted trees for decades, especially on Arbor Day. (*Arbor* is Latin for *tree*.) In most states, this special tree-planting day is observed on the last Friday in April.

It is fun to plant young seedlings or saplings, to care for them, and to watch them grow. The results, after many years, are large trees that cast shade and that provide shelter and food for birds, squirrels, and other wildlife.

Now kids all over North America are planting more trees than ever before. They have learned about the importance of trees, both locally and globally.

In cities and suburbs, trees act as natural summertime air conditioners. Their shade helps keep buildings, sidewalks, streets, and parked cars cool. Trees reduce the need to burn fuels to produce electricity that runs air conditioners. By blocking winter winds, they reduce heating costs.

Trees also remove ozone, dust particles, and other pollutants from the air. Furthermore, they absorb carbon dioxide gas. Some of the carbon from this gas becomes part of a tree's structure. A fast-growing tree can absorb 25 pounds of

carbon dioxide each year. If not cut down, trees can store lots of carbon for many years.

The amount of carbon dioxide in the air is increasing. It is added to the atmosphere when coal, gasoline, and other fuels are burned. Cutting down and burning trees also adds carbon dioxide to air. This worries scientists who study the earth's atmosphere. They believe that adding more and more carbon dioxide to our air will make temperatures rise all over the world.

This is called global warming. Rising temperatures and drought could cause crops to fail and many plants and animals to become extinct. A warming atmosphere could also cause glaciers and polar ice caps to melt, raising sea levels and threatening people who live along coasts. If global warming becomes a reality, it could be the most serious of all threats to our environment.

One important way to halt global warming is to reduce levels of carbon dioxide. People can help by cutting down no more trees than necessary. They also can plant young trees that will store carbon for many years to come.

Thousands of kids are planting trees—in rural and suburban areas, and in grim, treeless areas of big cities. As the result of an Urban Woodlands Project, trees have been planted on vacant lots in two New York City boroughs, Brooklyn and the Bronx. (This project is sponsored by Environmental Action Coalition, a nonprofit organization that works to improve the quality of life in New York City.)

Through this project public school students in the fourth, fifth, and sixth grades study the history of the area. They learn which plants and wild animals once lived there. They take walks to discover what lives there now. They observe that the squirrels, birds, and other wildlife they see depend on existing trees and bushes in their neighborhood.

Then they add to the wildlife habitat on "planting day," but other steps come first. There's much more to planting trees than sticking a seedling or sapling in the ground. The site must be a good, long-term place for trees, not one where they are likely to be cut down. Many communities have laws that affect tree planting. Planting trees may require city permits or authorization from the parks department, as well as permission from individual landowners if the planting site is not public space. (The adult leaders of the Urban Woodlands Project helped with these steps.)

Sixth-graders in one school received permission to work on a lot where a lone pine tree grew. First they got rid of discarded trash, including disposable diapers (which the kids called "the worst part" of the project). Then they improved the soil with peat moss and fertilizer before planting trees.

A city forester gave advice on the kinds of trees that used to live in the area. The city parks department provided the young trees and shrubs for planting day: junipers, white pines, American beeches, and shrubs called witch hazel. An eleven-year-old boy said, "Planting day was like all the sixth-graders fixing New York."

For several years after planting, trees may need watering and other care. Kids in succeeding classes care for the trees and try to keep the little forests free of litter. They also plant native wildflowers among the trees.

Some environments, such as deserts and prairies, are naturally treeless. Planting trees in these areas may do more harm than good. It is always best to plant trees and shrubs

that are native to a region. They support native birds, insects, and other wildlife better than "alien" plants.

In Florida ten kids in a 4-H club asked for tree seedlings from a local garden club and from their state Division of Forestry. In their area of northeastern Florida, the native trees included oaks, sweet gum, and sycamore. For a year they cared for the seedlings in a nursery. Then in 1990 on Arbor Day (which is observed in late January in Florida), the kids planted a hundred young trees.

The club members have planted many more since then. They live in an area where houses and shopping malls are replacing trees. Josh, an eleven-year-old, said, "I didn't like what the developers were doing to my hometown, and I'm glad that I can help with my trees."

One sapling, or even a hundred, cannot be expected to affect the earth's atmosphere. But thousands of kids are planting trees. Millions of trees, allowed to grow tall, can make a difference in the world.

Planting Tips

Once you have permission to plant young trees or shrubs on school grounds, park land, a vacant lot, or another site, think about the number and kinds of plants that will be right for the land. Use plants that you have learned are native to your area.

Remember that many kinds of trees need lots of space both above- and belowground when they are fully grown. As the years pass, their roots and limbs will need room to spread. Don't plant them close to buildings. If wires or other obstructions loom overhead, choose plants that do not grow tall. Also, resist the temptation to plant several tree saplings close together. In a decade or two they may be so crowded together that their growth will be stunted.

The plants themselves often can be obtained free from city and county governments or parks departments. Small numbers might be donated by a plant nursery. These organizations might also be sources of tools, advice, and supervision; and they might help with heavy labor.

The best time to plant trees and shrubs is in the early spring or in the fall. Once you have picked an actual spot for planting, dig a small hole a foot or more deep to test the soil's water drainage. If drainage is poor, the plants' roots may rot. Fill the hole with water. If it drains out within 12 hours, the drainage is okay. You can improve drainage by digging the planting hole deeper than needed and filling the extra bottom space with stones or gravel.

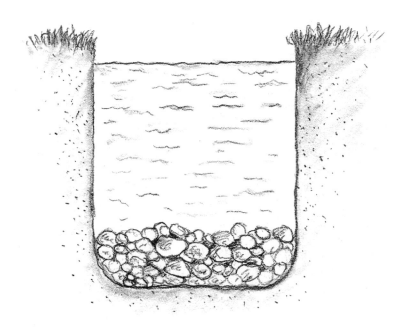

A key to the survival of tree saplings and other plants is making sure that the planting hole is wide and deep enough. There must be room for roots to set in their natural position, and later to spread. The hole should be a foot deeper than the height of the roots and twice as wide as the

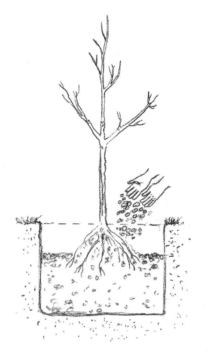

span of the roots. Loosening the soil on the sides and bottom of the hole will allow root tips to grow easily and will also help drainage.

After placing the sapling or other young plant upright in the hole, begin to shovel soil around the roots. Press it in firmly to support the plant and to remove large air pockets. Pour plenty of water into the hole when it is three-quarters filled with soil. Water again after adding more soil. The water helps bring soil particles in direct contact with roots and gives the plant a good start in its new home. Frequent watering in the following weeks is vital.

If rainfall is scarce, the tree may need further watering during the spring, summer, and fall of its first growing season. Adding a three-inch layer of such mulch as wood chips, peat moss, or leaf mold around the base of the trunk will help keep the soil moist. Until its trunk grows strong, a young tree may also need loose support from stakes and wires so that it is held upright but can still sway in the wind.

For further information about tree planting, write to these organizations whose addresses are given at the end of this book: Global Releaf, National Arbor Day Foundation, and Tree People.

2

Saving Rain Forests

Many years ago a penny was valuable. You could buy candy, or even a toy, with just a few pennies. Now a penny seems almost worthless. A hundred pennies is worth a dollar—still not much money. Nevertheless, if you keep saving your pennies, and pennies that others don't want, those little nuisance coins can add up.

In Grand Rapids, Michigan, elementary and junior high students at St. Andrew's School collected more than 20,000 pennies. That's two hundred dollars. It would have bought a lot of candy. Instead, it bought eight acres of rain forest in Costa Rica, preserving the forest as wildlife habitat. (An acre of land is about the size of a football field.)

The children's fund-raising effort was called "Pennies for Pythons and Parrots." It was a Tree Amigos project. *Amigos* means "friends" in Spanish. Tree Amigos programs involve being friends to trees. They also promote friendship between people in the United States and people in Latin America. (To learn more about Tree Amigos and other environmental groups, see "Where to Get More Information" on page 61.)

Students in another school in Grand Rapids are also Tree Amigos. They have raised money by staging musicals, including one called "Rain Forest Review." With their earnings they also bought rain forest land in Costa Rica.

The idea for this special rain forest came from a school boy in Sweden. In 1987 Sharon Kinsman, a biology professor from Bates College in Maine, who studies the lives of rain forests, showed pictures of tropical rain forests to students in a Swedish elementary classroom. The students learned about the rich variety of plants and animals that live in rain forests. They also learned that these forests are being destroyed. Worldwide, millions of acres are cut and burned each year.

Later Sharon remarked, "Sweden is a place where most people—especially children—respond with their hearts to anything about forests." In that classroom, nine-year-old Roland Tiensuu asked, "Why can't we earn money to help buy a rain forest park?"

"You can!" said Sharon, for she knew of a group that was buying forest land in the area of Costa Rica's Monteverde Rain Forest. Then it cost only $25 an acre. (By 1993 the cost of an acre of unspoiled forest there had risen to $100.)

Encouraged by Sharon and by their teacher, Eha Kern, the children in that class wrote a play about rain forests. The money they charged for admission to the play went into a fund for buying rain forest land. High school students and others pitched in. They raised money by doing chores for people, making and selling T-shirts, and asking for donations. Soon the students in just one small Swedish school had raised enough money to buy 15 acres of the Monteverde forest.

Since then, schoolchildren in several nations have raised enough money to save thousands of acres of threatened rain forest in Costa Rica. The kids do not actually own the land. The money they raise is forwarded to the Monteverde Conservation League. This nonprofit group has purchased more than 35,000 acres known as Bosque Eterno de los Ninos (The Children's Eternal Forest).

Even though they don't directly own the land, children feel connected to the forest and its animals. Sharon Kinsman said, "They talk about *my* forest, *my* resplendent quetzals, *my* golden toads. They have a sense of pride and responsibility."

Lots of young people want to actually visit the rain forest and learn about it in person. So, in addition to buying more land, the Monteverde Conservation League hopes that someday it can build facilities where visitors can stay.

An international network of children's rain forest organizations is establishing similar rain forest preserves in other countries. They have helped establish or expand other forest preserves in Thailand, Belize, Ecuador, and Costa Rica. Meanwhile, more than 14,000 acres remain in Costa Rica that could be added to the Children's Eternal Forest.

Outside this preserve, most of the forest has been cleared and is used as pasture for cattle. In other areas, tropical forests are cut for their timber and are not replanted. This is a double blow to the environment. The first blow is the loss of millions of trees that once stored carbon. Often the trees are burned, and many tons of carbon dioxide are released into the air, adding to the problem of global warming.

Even worse is the second blow to the environment: the loss of the rich variety of plants and animals that thrive in tropical forests. In Costa Rica alone, more than 1,100 kinds of orchids have been found. Thousands of insects and other animals live in the treetops of tropical forests.

Millions of unnamed living things live on Earth, and many of these species exist only in tropical forests. When the forests are destroyed, so are the creatures that depend on them.

Saving forests everywhere, and especially saving tropical forests, is one of the most important efforts young people can make on behalf of the environment. They can help by raising money in many ways. Some classes hold bake sales. Some kids contribute a month's allowance or money they received as a birthday or holiday gift. And some simply save pennies.

Fund-Raising Tips

Whether you aim to save several acres of tropical rain forest or raise money for another project to help the environment, here are tips on fund-raising. Each of them, to varying degrees, requires permission and help from parents, teachers, or other adults.

—In ten states, used beverage cans and bottles can be collected for the refund of deposit fees. Many people discard these cans and bottles, and in certain areas, such as parks and picnic areas, hundreds can be gathered.

—Bake sales are a proven way for one classroom or a larger group to raise money. Timing and publicity are important. Avoid close competition with another bake sale and use posters and notices to parents to advertise the sale *and* the project you want them to support. (Be sure to help prepare the baked goods, too!)

—Creating and selling a cookbook is a more ambitious project. Decisions have to be made about the number of recipes, their sources, the amount you charge for the cookbook, and how it will be made—its paper, illustrations, cover, and how the pages are held together. The number of cookbooks to be printed depends mostly on who you want to sell them to—teachers, parents, and relatives associated with the students of one school, or perhaps to a whole community. Selling a cookbook to the entire town may raise more money but will also require more work in publicizing it.

The simplest way to gather recipes is to ask parents and teachers for a favorite. Instead of a general cookbook, though, it could consist of only dessert recipes. In Bridgewater, New Jersey, a fifth-grade class compiled a cookbook called *Tropical Treats* by writing to the ambassadors of several countries that have rain forests. (The money they raised was used to help native people who rely on rain forests for their livelihood.)

—Car washes and T-shirt sales are other ways to raise money for your project. Both require considerable help from parents and other adults. Think about the qualities of your school or community population when you consider different ways of raising funds—what works in one area may fail in another.

3

Wild Places and Wildlife

In Lexington, Kentucky, students at Deep Springs Elementary School raised money to help buy a section of wild land. The land, however, was not in the faraway tropics. It was in their own state, in a special area called the Thompson Creek Glades.

In preparation for Earth Day, 1990, the students had studied different habitats. A habitat is a plant-animal community in which a certain organism lives. For example, large grassy areas are the habitat of the American bison.

The children were surprised to learn that herds of bison once roamed their state. Open prairies once covered more than two million acres of Kentucky. Now there are no bison roaming free in Kentucky, but scattered remnants of the prairies still remain.

One such place is Thompson Creek Glades. Mixed in with forested areas are grassy openings where unusual glade and prairie plants grow. Some of the plants are rare in Kentucky. They include reindeer lichen, silky aster, and Indian paintbrush. Butterflies, mice, songbirds, foxes, deer, and other wildlife also thrive in this habitat.

In 1990 the Kentucky chapter of the Nature Conservancy, a conservation group, was buying 171 acres to establish the Thompson Creek Glades Preserve. The land cost about $575 an acre, and the students of Deep Springs School set that amount as their goal.

Their school had a machine for making display buttons. The kids made buttons bearing the message "Save the Wildlife" and sold them for $1.50 each. As their fund grew closer and closer to their goal, all of the elementary students made posters and bumper stickers, and wrote essays about the project. They were competing for a chance to visit the glades for a special ceremony.

On Earth Day the winning students from each grade rode on a bus to the Thompson Creek Glades Preserve. There they were led on a hike and shown some of the rare plants. They learned that a few years earlier this rare habitat had almost been destroyed by a landfill. And, most importantly, they presented their school's "Save the Wildlife" fund to the director of the Kentucky Nature Conservancy. Their efforts helped ensure that all 171 acres of the preserve were saved.

These kids from Kentucky had to take a long bus ride to the nature preserve they helped save. Some students are fortunate to have a natural area on or near their school grounds. Some help create one.

In Encinitas, California, a biology teacher dreamed of transforming a quarter-acre plot of land by the high school science building into a desert garden. High school students helped make the dream a reality.

They pulled weeds, laid trails, dug holes, and planted cacti and other desert plants native to the area. The students also established a nursery for rare desert plants.

Beginning in 1986, sixth-grade students of Westwood School in Casper, Wyoming, "adopted" part of a creek in their area. It is Bolton Creek, a spring-fed stream that winds its way through the dry landscape.

At floodtime the creek overflows and erodes its banks. To help reduce erosion, all of the students were asked to bring discarded Christmas trees to school. The sixth-graders placed the trees where they would slow water running off the land and thereby reduce erosion.

The following spring the boys and girls researched which species of plants would grow well along the stream banks. In May, armed with shovels and water buckets, they planted 300 fruit-bearing trees and shrubs that provide food for wildlife.

The sixth-graders graduated from Westwood School that spring and began attending another school in the fall of 1987. Before graduating, however, the class decided to draw up a will. They passed on the Bolton Creek project to the next sixth-grade class. Everyone signed the will, and it was presented to the fifth grade at a special assembly. A "key" to Bolton Creek's future was also given to the fifth-graders.

The tradition has continued. Each new sixth-grade class at the Westwood School inherits that key, and with it the goal of improving habitat along Bolton Creek. The students have built small dams that slow stream flow and trap sediments. They wrapped wire fencing around the trunks of cottonwood trees, protecting them from being felled by beavers. They also have planted many young cottonwoods.

These native trees shade the water, and their roots help prevent erosion. They are important streamside trees in the arid West.

"We have made Bolton Creek a better place," said one sixth-grader. Students in the lower grades look forward to their chance to improve the stream valley habitat of Bolton Creek.

In some places, a habitat is perfect for certain wild animals except for one key aspect. In the case of bluebirds, that vital element is a place to nest and raise young. The numbers of bluebirds (eastern, western, and mountain species) in North America have declined. Bluebirds usually nest inside natural hollows, or cavities chipped out by woodpeckers, in trees at the edge of open fields.

Different kinds of birds often compete for a nesting site in a tree. Bluebirds usually lose to the more aggressive starlings, a non-native species. Fortunately, bluebirds will build nests in specially-made birdhouses. An entrance hole exactly one and one-half inches in diameter lets bluebirds in but keeps starlings out.

Bluebirds are making a comeback in some areas, thanks to the efforts of young people. Kids in schools, Boy Scouts, Girl Scouts, and 4-H clubs are building bluebird houses. This is a good indoor project for the fall and winter months. Then they put up the houses in winter or early spring, before the bluebirds return from the south.

Picking the right bluebird habitat is important. Open areas with scattered trees are best. Kids have fastened bluebird houses on trees or posts in parks, campgrounds, golf courses, and cemeteries. Sometimes years pass before migrating bluebirds find the houses. Sooner or later, the

kids who built the houses get to watch bluebirds raise their young. Then they have the satisfaction of helping the bluebird population grow.

Bluebirds are appealing creatures, but other, less-popular wild animals are also being helped by young people. Bats, for example, seem ugly and even dangerous to many people. But scientists and others who know them understand that bats are usually harmless and that they help control insect populations. In North America bats eat tons of night-flying insects, including mosquitoes.

In 1987 Debra Rust, a teacher in a Birmingham, Alabama, elementary school, learned about the great value of bats.

She shared her enthusiasm for bats with some of her students. One girl, Janie Miller, said, "Let's form our own bat club and start saving bats in Alabama!"

Soon the B.A.T. Club was formed. The name stands for "Bats Aren't Terrible; Bats Are Terrific." By 1994 the club had more than a thousand members. Many were students at the school where the club started, but parents and boys and girls from other schools also have joined.

One goal of the B.A.T. Club is simply to spread the truth about bats. Club members do this by giving programs at other schools, making posters and bumper stickers, and appearing on radio and television programs. Their school's superintendent said, "In 27 years in education, I have never seen such a complete 'attitude turnaround' as I have observed with these youngsters as they taught teachers, students, and parents in the school system and community that bats . . . are friends and preservers of our environment."

B.A.T. Club members write letters to political leaders in support of bat conservation. When a housing development

threatened local bats, the club's letters, plus a visit to the mayor's office, caused some changes in the plans. Nothing was built near a cave where endangered gray bats roosted.

In some areas bats face the same problem as bluebirds. They are scarce because they lack the right kind of shelter. B.A.T. Club members have sold bumper stickers to raise money to buy bat houses. These specially designed houses give bats a place to rest during the day.

The B.A.T. Club has given bat houses to nature centers, the Birmingham Zoo, and the Birmingham Botanical Gardens. Even if the houses attract no bats, they draw the attention of human visitors. Many people are surprised to learn that bats are such desirable wildlife.

The B.A.T. Club continues to spread the word that "Bats Aren't Terrible; Bats Are Terrific."

Tips on Saving Wildlife

—If adopting a section of a stream is a possible project in your area, you can get useful information from the Izaak Walton League of America (1401 Wilson Blvd., Arlington, VA 22209). This environmental organization provides brochures and an information kit as part of its Save Our Streams program. Some actions suggested for helping the life in a stream environment can also improve wildlife habitat along the edge of a pond.

—You can "adopt" other kinds of habitats, too, with the aim of making them more attractive to wildlife. Some school properties include areas of forest, unused open land, or other habitats. The first step is to study the plants and animals that now use the habitat. For example, which species of birds feed, rest, or nest there?

Once you have permission to make changes, another step might be to clear a nature trail that winds through the habitat and makes it easier for school classes and others to see the wild plants and animals. (Such a trail also can help to prevent people from scaring animals or trampling on plants.) To make the area more attractive to wild animals, think of their basic needs: food, water, shelter, and space. Sometimes the arrangement of these resources can be a key factor. For example, shrubs or other plants growing near a bird feeder or birdbath attract more birds than those without plants. The shrubs give birds shelter and a safe place to wait near the water or feeder.

A dead tree can be a lively place, serving as shelter for birds and small mammals that nest or hide in holes, and as a home and a food source for many insects and other small creatures. Certain kinds of trees, shrubs, and other plants attract a variety of animals because of the nuts, berries, or seeds they produce. For more information, write to the National Wildlife Federation (1400 16th Street, N.W., Washington, DC 20036) and ask about its Backyard Wildlife Habitat program.

—You can even create a garden full of plants whose flowers attract butterflies to feed, and others upon which their caterpillars feed. You will need a sunny spot. Butterflies and the plants that entice them need at least six hours of sunlight each day. A shallow pan of water set on the ground also gives butterflies a drinking place. Among the flowers that attract butterflies are: aster, cornflower, marigold, strawflower, zinnia, butterfly weed, coreopsis, phlox, and honeysuckle. Each species of butterfly has a favorite kind of plant on which its caterpillars feed. They include: aster, spicebush, milkweed, thistle, clover, Queen Anne's lace, goldenrod, and wild lupine. (For more information, write to Butterfly Gardeners Association, 1021 North Main Street, Allentown, PA 18104.)

—If you live near an area of good bluebird habitat (see page 32), building and putting up wooden houses specially suited for them can help increase the numbers of these beautiful members of the thrush family. Bluebird houses should be cleaned between nestings, so you should be able to open the top, front, or a side. For instructions on how to build a bluebird house, contact a local cooperative extension office or write to the North American Bluebird Society, Box 6295, Silver Spring, MD 20906.

4

Up, Up, and Away— to Where?

Everything was ready. Hundreds of brightly colored balloons had been inflated with helium, a gas that is lighter than air. At a signal, the balloons were released. The crowd cheered at the spectacle. The balloons sailed away, rising higher and higher until they looked like little specks in the sky. Then they disappeared. Where do such balloons go? Most of them rise about five miles and then explode. As they rise higher and higher into the atmosphere, the air gets thinner. The helium in the balloon expands, and the latex stretches until it bursts. Bits of rubber fall as litter to the land or waters below.

Some balloons lose part of their helium before they rise very far. They may sail on the wind for hundreds of miles. Eventually they settle back to the earth's surface.

Because people enjoy balloon launches, no one objected to this sort of littering. Then, in 1985, a whale washed up on a New Jersey shore. It died. Scientists found a balloon blocking the passageway between the whale's stomach and intestines. It appeared that the whale had been unable to digest food. However, scientists could not say for certain whether the balloon had caused the whale's death.

The balloon was made of mirrorlike Mylar™ material. In 1987 another kind of balloon was found blocking the digestive tract of a dead sea turtle. It was made of latex rubber, and the balloon was the kind that is usually filled with helium and released, or escapes by accident, to soar away in the sky.

Again, scientists could not prove, or disprove, that the balloon had caused the turtle's death. But marine biologists became concerned. They know that sea turtles eat jellyfish. The turtles sometimes mistake plastic bags for jellyfish and have died from eating them. A latex balloon, floating on the ocean's surface, also might look like a jellyfish. If a sea turtle were to eat it, the balloon might cause the turtle to starve to death.

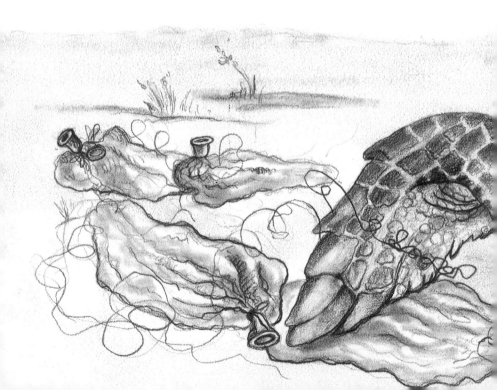

People began to question the wisdom of balloon launches. Some schools and communities canceled these events. Balloon makers and sellers protested. They said there was no proof that any animal had been killed by a balloon.

This was true, at least as of 1993. But the oceans are vast. Each year scores of sea turtles could die from eating balloons and sink to the bottom. We would never know it. "No proof" does not necessarily mean that balloons do no harm to sea turtles or other marine life.

Environmental groups now oppose balloon launches. The National Park Service banned launches and stopped selling latex balloons in the national parks. Young people campaign against balloon launches in many areas.

In Redding, California, two sisters, ages 7 and 10, learned that their school was planning to release balloons.

They told their teachers and principal about the possible danger to sea life. The launch was canceled.

A fourth-grade girl in a New Hampshire school also spoke up against balloon launches. She helped form a group called the Balloon Launching Terminators. With the support of several teachers, the group persuaded the school to ban balloon launches.

At its Earth Day 1990 celebration, an elementary school in western New York substituted pigeons for balloons. A man who raises homing pigeons brought a flock to the school. The boys and girls were excited to see the birds fly into the sky, circle around, then head for home.

That same year a fifth-grade class in a Kent, Ohio, school wrote letters to officials in a nearby city, urging them to call off a balloon launch. Believe it or not, balloons released in the Midwest can reach the ocean. In just two days, a balloon let go in Ohio had blown all the way to the Atlantic Ocean coast at South Carolina.

The kids' effort failed to stop that city's balloon release. But schoolchildren in other communities have influenced their political leaders. Several cities have passed laws against balloon launches or prohibit them under antilitter laws. Florida, Connecticut, and Tennessee have banned or restricted the release of helium-filled balloons. Letters from kids helped make these changes happen.

Tips on Influencing Authorities

Whether you seek to change the way things are done in your school or in local, state, or national government, remember that there is strength in numbers. The greater the number of names on a petition or of letters written by different people, the better the chances for success. Also, doing solid research on the issue is vital in order to propose specific changes *and* to be taken seriously.

Political leaders can sometimes be influenced by calls and letters from citizens, including kids who are future voters. Sometimes it is tempting to write an angry letter, complete with sarcasm and name-calling, but this is not likely to get the results you want. Also avoid a "preachy" tone. Treat the person you are writing to as a potential ally. A respectful letter that demonstrates that you have a good understanding of the issue or issues involved will be more effective.

Be personal. Say who you are and why you care. To aid your own credibility, you might include details that show that you understand the views of those who disagree with you. Be as specific as possible about what you want the person to do.

It is important to address your letter to the person who has the power to make the change you want. Below are some United States government addresses you might need. A reference librarian can help you locate the address of the local mayor, a town councilperson, a county official in your county's government, or the governor or legislators in your state's capital.

President_____
The White House
1600 Pennsylvania Avenue, NW
Washington, DC 20500

5

Reading, 'Riting, 'Rithmetic, and Recycling

Balloons are just a tiny part of the big environmental problem usually called solid waste. Everything people throw away—including garbage, newspapers, cans, and bottles—is part of this problem. Young people all over the nation are working to help solve it.

Sometimes, what is needed is simply to clean up the mess that others leave. This is especially true along beaches. Litter on lake and ocean beaches not only looks ugly but it can harm wildlife. Birds and crabs become entangled in snarls of discarded fishing line. Ducks and other birds also get stuck in the plastic rings that once held six-packs of cans.

One environmental group, The Center for Marine Conservation, each year leads a big beach cleanup in several nations. On a special day in September, thousands of volunteers—including young people—collect tons of litter and trash from beaches. In 1993 more than 220,000 volunteers from 36 U.S. states and territories and 37 countries worked on more than 5,600 miles of beaches and waterways. They picked up more than 2,400 tons of debris.

Cleaning up after careless people is, unfortunately, steady

work. Some groups of kids patrol beaches for litter several times a year.

Fourth- and fifth-graders at Ocean City Elementary School in Maryland formed a group called STOP. The name stands for "Students Tackle Ocean Plastic." They have sponsored cleanup days at the Assateague National Seashore. They also prepared information sheets on the dangers of plastic debris to wildlife. Then they handed out more than 1,600 of these sheets to visitors at a boat show.

Solid waste problems exist in other places besides just beaches. Kids face them every day at school and at home. In fact, some young people really begin to understand the size of the solid waste problem when they keep a record of everything they throw away in one day.

Some Ohio third-graders kept a tally of their "daily garbage output" in school. In one day, nine kids threw away 109 pieces of solid waste. The total included plastic bags, paper napkins, juice boxes, soda bottles, plastic forks, dead batteries, scrap paper, orange peels, apple cores, and candy wrappers.

That was just the waste at school. The tally of discarded items rises much higher if you keep track of a family's garbage output for a day. In the early 1990s, each person in the United States threw away an average of eight pounds of stuff each day. No wonder landfills are overflowing.

Landfills, where solid wastes are buried, are ugly, smelly places. Often, harmful wastes in landfills get into underground water supplies. No one wants a landfill in their neighborhood. So very few new landfills are being opened.

Where can the solid wastes go? Many communities are trying to make their landfills last longer by reducing the amount of trash that needs to be buried. Cities, towns, and counties in several states collect newspaper, glass, and other items for recycling.

The process of recycling items into new products is fascinating. In some school districts students take field trips to collection centers for recycling or to plants where recycling actually occurs. They see the huge amounts of newsprint, glass, and other materials that are collected. And they learn how so-called waste is made into useful products again.

Recycling has a positive effect on the environment, and it's something kids can do right at home or in school.

In 1989 some elementary school students from Nebraska began to recycle plastic milk jugs. They learned that a recycling center in a neighboring town collected these jugs.

They also learned that the plastic in such jugs can be made into toys, coat hangers, flowerpots, and plastic lumber. By the spring of 1990, kids in all grades of the Silver Lake Elementary School were bringing in plastic jugs as well as tin cans. More than three thousand jugs were recycled. Even more were collected the following year. Then the kids added discarded envelopes to their recycling efforts.

When kids learn that they have the power to help the environment, one successful project often leads to another, and another. For example, the students of one grade or the members of an ecology club might get their whole school to collect aluminum cans for recycling.

Then they might persuade the school administration to print exams and letters to parents on both sides of sheets of paper. This conserves paper. Schools use lots of paper, and much of it can be collected after use for recycling, too. As a next step, kids can urge their schools to *buy* new paper that is made wholly or partly from recycled paper.

This is an important step. Recycling companies will succeed and grow if schools, businesses, and other customers buy their products. This can lead to lower costs for the products. It also encourages companies to set up networks of recycling collection centers. (In 1993 the United States government took this big step when President Bill Clinton ordered all federal agencies, by 1995, to buy paper containing at least 20 percent recycled material. The amount must increase to 30 percent by 1999, and the recycled material cannot be scraps from paper mills but must be paper already used by people.)

In Longview, Texas, the seniors of the Trinity School chose to have their yearbook printed on recycled paper. Nationwide, twelve million high school yearbooks are printed each year. Every high school has an opportunity to choose recycled paper for its yearbook.

Besides recycling, another way to reduce solid waste is to throw away fewer things. Kids have written letters to companies that make throwaway cameras, razors, and flashlights. They urge them to stop producing these wasteful objects, which cannot be recycled. In this way, they try to

stop solid waste at its source, rather than after it is manufactured, used, and discarded.

In many schools, teachers each day drink coffee or tea
from paper or plastic foam cups, which they discard. Kids
in hundreds of schools have persuaded teachers to use
ceramic mugs that can be rinsed and used again and again.

In schools all over North America, students have cam-
paigned to rid their cafeterias of plastic foam cups (and
sometimes trays and plates made from the same material).
These cups are made from petroleum. They break down
very slowly in landfills. Until 1988 some plastic foam cups
were manufactured in a process that used CFC gases. These
gases harm a layer of ozone, high above the earth, that
shields all life from powerful ultraviolet sun rays.

Even though plastic foam cups are no longer made with
CFC gases, some people think they should not be used.
However, students who have studied different kinds of cups
have learned that paper cups also harm the environment.

Paper cups are made of wood chips from trees.
Compared with the manufacture of a plastic foam cup, the
process of making a paper one takes more raw material,
uses much more energy, and produces much more waste
water. Also, paper cups coated with wax or a plastic film
cannot be recycled. They decay slowly in landfills.

Choosing cups or other products that do the least harm
to our environment can be difficult. Some environmental
problems have no easy answers. Young people have to gather information and learn a lot before urging others to take
action.

The most important lesson they learn, however, is that

their actions really do make a difference in reducing solid wastes and other threats to our environment.

Tips on Reducing Solid Wastes

—Start at home. If you live in an area where recycling some materials—perhaps newspapers, cans, bottles—is required, make sure that your own family follows the law. If you have a yard or garden, you can reduce the wastes collected from your house even more by starting a compost pile. Composting is the natural process of allowing organic (once living) materials to gradually decay into rich, fertile soil. Some organic stuff, such as meat, bones, and dairy products, should not be put in compost; but you can mix together lawn clippings, leaves, eggshells, and fruit and vegetable waste. Most books and magazines about gardening give helpful information about starting and maintaining a compost pile.

—Another way to reduce solid wastes in your own home is to buy certain products and avoid buying others. For example, the recycling programs in some areas accept certain kinds of plastic containers but not others. Some communities collect plastic containers with a 1, 2, or 3 in the recycling symbol visible on their·bottoms, but they do not accept those marked with higher numbers. Your family can check the numbers before buying and purchase the products packaged in recyclable plastic. Also try to avoid buying items that include a lot of instant-waste packaging. (Unfortunately, many toys are packaged this way!)

—Recycling efforts vary greatly from state to state, and from school to school. Investigate the recycling programs of your school, community, and state. Can more be done? You

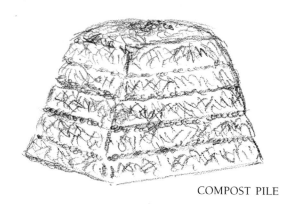

COMPOST PILE

COMPOSTING CONTAINER

KITCHEN COMPOST
BUCKET

SOIL SAVER

may learn that environmental organizations are already active, trying to strengthen the recycling effort in your community or state. For example, does your state government purchase new paper with at least 20 percent of its content provided by recycled paper? If not, you and your classmates can write letters urging support of this policy that is now followed by the federal government.

Closer to home, see if the recycling program in your own school can be improved. Remember, your school's principal may not have the authority to make some changes. Your task may be to persuade a school district superintendent or school board. Whatever change you propose, offer evidence from other schools where it has been successful. Being able to say, "This is working fine over at Nearby and Similar School" can be a key factor in bringing about change.

6

Kid Power

When her students studied environmental problems, sixth-grade teacher Diana Feingold found that they were concerned but felt frustrated. They were, after all, "just kids." They could not vote. They felt powerless.

With her encouragement, these students discovered that they *did* have the power to influence adults and to help solve environmental problems. One key, they found, was to get more and more young people involved.

That class of 18 students at River Trails Junior High School in Mount Prospect, Illinois, began by holding meetings after school. They formed a group they called Project P.E.O.P.L.E., which stands for People Educating Other People for a Long-Lasting Environment. By 1994 Project P.E.O.P.L.E. had more than 1,500 members in several states. Its motto is "Taking care of the earth is not a hobby, it is a responsibility."

The group's name is its aim. Members study environmental issues. They know about lots of things people can do in their own homes to help the environment. Members approach people at museums and other public places. They tell about their organization. They raise issues, ask and answer questions, and suggest solutions.

Project P.E.O.P.L.E. also gives awards to businesses and schools that adopt "environment-friendly" practices. For example, a bank might begin to collect its office waste paper for recycling. Stores and other businesses often don't need much urging to take such steps. They make "environment-friendly" changes and apply for the award. They want to display a Project P.E.O.P.L.E. plaque, which was designed by several kids who are members. The award is good public relations for a business or school. It is also a positive sign for the environment.

One girl was asked what she had learned from being a member. She said, "Before, we didn't think anyone would listen to us. Now we are confident that they will."

Project P.E.O.P.L.E. is one of dozens of groups that kids have formed in North America. Another is H.O.W. (Help Our World), founded by sixth-graders of the Mountain Park School in Berkeley Heights, New Jersey. In 1988 they were studying environmental problems ranging from global warming to noise pollution.

They were worried about the kind of world they would live in as adults. They expressed their concern in letters to state and national legislators. They also wrote to the "Letters to the Editor" section of local newspapers and made posters for display in store windows.

The H.O.W. motto is simply "You can make a difference." The group holds an annual "Environmental Awareness Night" in Berkeley Heights. And each year H.O.W. members take action to help improve the environment in their area, especially in their own community. In 1992, for instance, four H.O.W. members spoke at a meeting of the Berkeley Heights Township Committee, urging town government to start a battery-recycling program. H.O.W. member Elizabeth Regit explained that battery acid leaks out and seeps into the groundwater supply.

Young Environmentalists Petition Committee on Battery Recycling was the headline in a newspaper report on the meeting. This act by four H.O.W. kids helped the efforts of other concerned citizens and led to a county-wide battery-recycling program.

The girls and boys of H.O.W. base their efforts on careful research of the issues. One girl said, "I never realized how important this was. My parents didn't even know as much as we do. We all learned a lot."

In their efforts to teach others, most groups of concerned kids make up pamphlets or publish newsletters of important ideas and actions. In time for Earth Day 1990, students of The Philadelphia School (Philadelphia, Pennsylvania) made a calendar called "Protect Our Planet." The calendar was packed with "environmental facts and positive actions."

"Protect Our Planet" was designed, written, and illustrated by the school's sixth-, seventh-, and eighth-graders. One girl who worked on it said, "I thought it was going to be this kind of homemade thing that only our relatives would want, but it turned out so nice."

In fact, a publisher agreed to print 8,000 copies—on recycled paper, of course. Each year the students produced new calendars, with new facts, actions, and illustrations. Thousands of copies of the calendars were printed, sold, and hung in homes and offices. Each page reminded readers of steps they could take to help our environment.

Across the country families, schools, businesses, and town

APRIL
PROTECT OUR PLANET

SUN.	MON.	TUES.	WED.	THURS.	FRI.	SAT.
1	2	3	4	5	6	7
8	9	10	11	12	13	14
						SPRING BEGINS
15	16	17	18	19	20	21
22	23					
29	30	24	25	26	27	28

EARTH DAY
RECYCLE REMINDER
ARBOR DAY

PLANTING TREES IS GOOD FOR THE ENVIRONMENT

governments have made some "environment-friendly" changes. Parents, teachers, school principals, and even a president, have learned from concerned kids.

In November 1989, President George Bush was presenting the Environmental Youth Awards to winning groups or individuals from ten regions of the United States. (The awards have been given each year since 1971.) One award-winner was Allen Graves, a high school student from California. He had won because of his efforts to get recycling started in his school and community.

Allen asked the president, "Does your office recycle?"

President Bush replied, "I don't know."

"It should," Allen said. Eight months later the White House began to recycle cans and newspapers. A recycling program for the White House had been under study. Allen Graves's question helped make it a reality.

Allen Graves had bravely used his right to speak out. This right to speak freely is granted by the First Amendment to the Constitution of the United States. In the fall of 1987, a New Jersey teacher explored the issue of freedom of speech with his fifth-grade class. Teacher Nick Byrne and his 19 students never dreamed where their study of the First Amendment would lead.

One kid asked how they could use their right to free expression. Nick Byrne suggested that the class choose a topic that concerned them and write letters to newspapers about it. The kids chose pollution. They did some research

and began writing. They wrote to newspapers and political leaders. They also decided to create a group and call it Kids Against Pollution (KAP).

KAP began as a fifth-grade class of the Tenakill School in Closter, New Jersey. By 1994, there were over 1,200 chapters of Kids Against Pollution in the United States and other countries.

In Closter, one of KAP's first projects was to prepare a petition that asked the school board to stop use of plastic foam products in local schools. The school board agreed. KAP also led a successful protest against a nearby balloon launch, and succeeded in having recycled paper used throughout the Closter school system.

Kids from the Tenakill School have spoken at churches, synagogues, and schools, and to legislators in the state capitals of New Jersey and New York. One KAP class wrote an Environmental Bill of Rights. Kids Against Pollution has succeeded in having this proposed as an amendment to the constitutions of New Jersey and of the United States.

Each May, Kids Against Pollution holds an Environmental Rights Day in Closter. To raise funds, the kids sell baked goods, T-shirts, and games made from recyclable materials. They also give free workshops on environmental problems.

Along with thousands of other young people, KAP members know that environmental problems are not easy to solve. Just as cleaning up after litterbugs is steady work, the job of reducing pollution, conserving resources, and saving wildlife does not end.

These efforts are not wasted. Working together, young people like yourself have the power to help and inspire everyone to take better care of the earth.

Where to Get More Information

Listed below are a few of many groups working for better care of our environment. Some, run mostly by kids, have programs aimed especially at young people. Others have such programs as part of their overall effort.

Some of these organizations are major national groups. Small groups with limited budgets are marked with an asterisk (*). When writing to these groups for information, please enclose a stamped, self-addressed business-sized envelope.

Audubon Activist
National Audubon Society
700 Broadway
New York, New York 10003
Ask for subscription information and a sample issue of this publication. It reports on environmental issues about which people may want to write letters or take other action.

Bat Conservation International
P. O. Box 162603
Austin, Texas 78716

Center for Marine Conservation
1725 DeSales Street, NW
Washington, D.C. 20036

*The Children's Rain Forest U.S.
P.O. Box 936
Lewiston, Maine 04240

*Earth Force
1501 Wilson Boulevard
Twelfth Floor
Arlington, Virginia 22209

Global ReLeaf
American Forests
P.O. Box 2000
Washington, D.C. 20013

*Help Our World (H.O.W.)
Columbia Middle School
345 Plainfield Avenue
Berkeley Heights, New Jersey
07922

*Kids Against Pollution
P.O. Box 22
Newport, New York 13416

*Kids for a Clean Environment
P.O. Box 158254
Nashville, Tennessee 37215

*Kids for Saving Earth Worldwide
P.O. Box 421118
Plymouth, Minnesota
55442

National Arbor Day Foundation
100 Arbor Avenue
Nebraska City, Nebraska 68410

National Wildlife Federation
1400 Sixteenth Street, NW
Washington, D.C. 20036-2266

The Nature Conservancy
1815 North Lynn Street
Arlington, Virginia 22209
The Nature Conservancy works to preserve special wild habitats in all states and abroad. From its main office you can get the address of nearby chapters and learn of projects that need funds and volunteer workers.

North American Bluebird Society
P.O. Box 6295
Silver Spring, Maryland 20906
Write for membership information as well as advice on building bluebird houses and placing them in habitats preferred by bluebirds.

*Project P.E.O.P.L.E.
P.O. Box 932
Prospect Heights, Illinois 60070

Rain Forest Action Network
450 Sansome Street
Suite 700
San Francisco, California 94111
Ask for a copy of the fact sheet that gives information on what to buy and what not to buy to help protect rain forests.

Renew America
1400 Sixteenth Street, NW
Suite 710
Washington, D.C. 20036
This organization identifies, promotes, and rewards successful environmental programs across the nation. Ask for the most recent copy of its "Environmental Success Index," which lists many groups, including those of young people, that can be contacted for more information.

Sierra Club
Attn: Information Dept.
730 Polk Street
San Francisco, California 94109
Ask for a list of available *What You Can Do* brochures and their costs. Subjects include ways to help save tropical forests and help solve solid waste problems.

Tree Amigos
Center for Environmental Study
143 Bostwick NE
Grand Rapids, Michigan 49509

Tree People
12601 Mulholland Drive
Beverly Hills, California 90210

The Wilderness Society
900 17th St. NW
Washington, D.C. 20006
This group specializes in issues involving land protection and biodiversity. Material specially designed for kids, *Saving Our Ancient Forests* ($4.00 includes S&H), Endangered Species Fact Sheet for Kids (free), and the Endangered Species Citizen Action Kits (free), can be requested by calling (202) 833-2300 or writing The Wilderness Society at the above address.

*Youth for Environmental Sanity
706 Frederick Street
Santa Cruz, California 95062
This group addresses high school assemblies, hosts summer camps, and presents workshops giving advice on how teenagers can help the environment. Much of the same information is in a 25-page booklet, *How to Have a Successful Environmental Club—A Student Action Guide* ($3.95, postage paid).

INDEX